# DINOSAURS UNITED

**LIGHTNING REX**
SPECIES: T. REX
POSITION: STRIKER

**COCO**
SPECIES: PTEROSAUR
POSITION: MIDFIELDER

**ZIGGY**
SPECIES: VELOCIRAPTOR
POSITION: MIDFIELDER

**SPIKE**
SPECIES: TRICERATOPS
POSITION: DEFENDER

**DIPPY**
SPECIES: DIPLODOCUS
POSITION: GOALIE

# *Cowardly Custard* PIRATE CREW

**CAPTAIN CUSTARD**
JOB: BOSS
POSITION: STRIKER

**SHIPMATE STUBBLE**
JOB: FIRST MATE
POSITION: MIDFIELDER

**MUGSY**
JOB: COOK
POSITION: MIDFIELDER

**SHIPMATE CLAW-DIA**
JOB: RIGGER
POSITION: DEFENDER

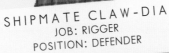

**BARNACLE**
JOB: CABIN BOY
POSITION: GOALIE

# EGMONT

*We bring stories to life*

First published in Great Britain 2017
by Egmont UK Limited,
The Yellow Building, 1 Nicholas Road, London W11 4AN
www.egmont.co.uk

Text copyright © Sam Hay 2017
Illustrations copyright © Daron Parton 2017

Sam Hay and Daron Parton have asserted their moral rights

ISBN 978 1 4052 7933 8

A CIP catalogue record for this title is available from the British Library

# DINOSAURS UNITED
### and the
### Cowardly Custard PIRATE CREW

Sam Hay

Daron Parton

EGMONT

Meet
# DINOSAURS UNITED –

Spike, Lightning Rex, Dippy, Ziggy and Coco are an awesome five-a-side football team who play in the Fantasy Football League.

They're **fast** and **fun** and always on the ball,
which is just as well because their opponents
use every sneaky trick in the book to
try to **win the Cup!**

Dinosaurs United were in a mega muddle. It was the day of the big football match against the Cowardly Custard Pirate Crew and the dinosaurs couldn't find their kit!

"My boots have vanished!"

"Where's my shirt?"

Lightning Rex called a **team meeting.**
"If we can't find our kit," he said.
"We **can't** play the match."

The
dinosaurs
gasped.

They'd never missed
a game before.

Just then something whizzed through the door.

"It's a message in a bottle," Lightning said.

"Let's see what it says . . ."

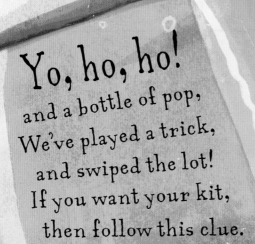

Yo, ho, ho!
and a bottle of pop,
We've played a trick,
and swiped the lot!
If you want your kit,
then follow this clue.
Yo, ho, ho!
from the
Cowardly Custard
Pirate Crew

Dinosaurs United groaned.
The sneaky pirates had pinched their football stuff!

"Wait!" said Spike. "There's a treasure map
on the back of the message."

"Looks like a map of our football pitch," said Dippy, "but what's that big **kiss** in the corner?"

Lightning laughed. "It's not a kiss. X marks the spot where we'll find our football kit. **Come on!**"

They raced onto the pitch . . .

"Ouch!"

"Ooo!"

"Yow!"

But someone had dumped an enormous pile of barnacle shells there!

"I bet Pirate Barnacle did this!" said Lightning.
"Quick, jump over the shells, like you're
leaping up for a header."

Dinosaurs United made it over the shells.
But they didn't get far . . .

# . . . . splat!

A large squishy ball burst all over Lightning.

"Water balloons!" he yelled.

Ziggy could see
who was firing at them.

"It's Shipmate Stubble!" she shouted.
"Hit the balloons back at him, like you're saving a goal!"

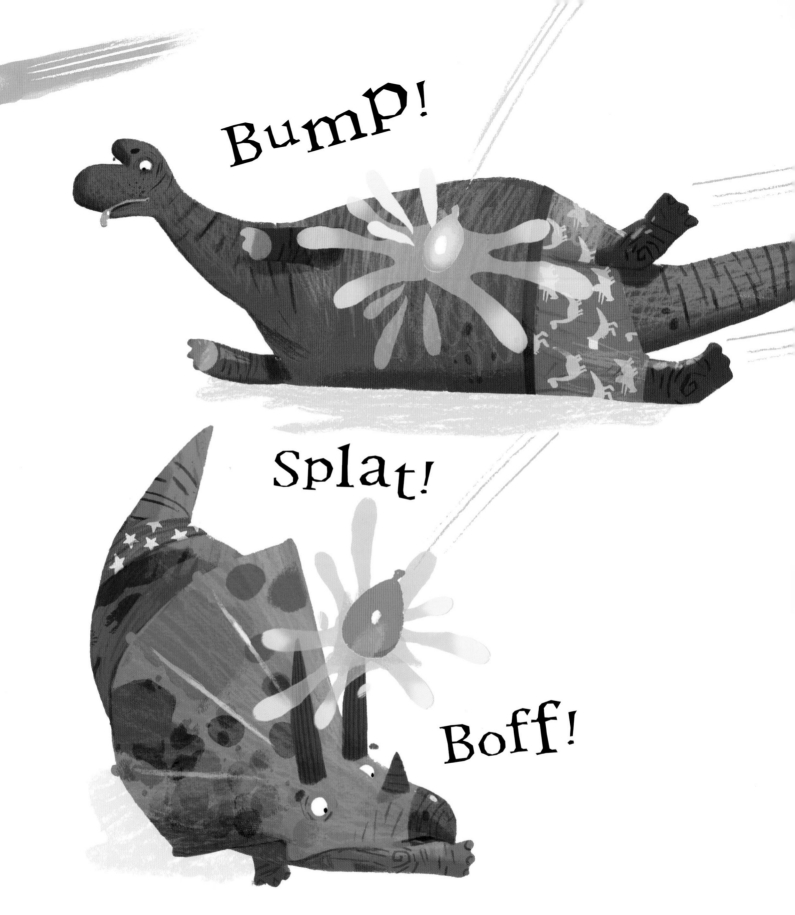

The dinosaurs made it past the cannon, but the pirates had more tricks up their salty sleeves . . .

Shipmate Claw-dia dashed past with
a sneaky grin on her face.

"Watch out!" Lightning yelled.

"Crabs!"

An army of nippy **crabs** was marching towards them.

"Ouch!"

Ziggy cried.

"One's got me."

"Hold on . . ." called Coco, and she lifted Ziggy up, while the rest of the dinosaurs dodged round the crabs.

"It's like **dribbling** in a match,"
Spike puffed. "But it's nearly time for
kick-off. We've got to find our kit!"

The dinosaurs **zoomed** down the pitch. But when they got to the end there was no sign of their kit.

Lightning scratched his scaly chin. "I don't understand it. All I can see is the half-time **snack trolley.**"

Dippy's tummy rumbled, "Custard doughnuts. Mmm!" He dived for the plate. But as he jumped, he bumped into the trolley and knocked it over . . .

"Whoah! Dippy,
you brain-o-saurus!"
Lightning shouted. "You found
our kit!"

Just then the referee blew his whistle.

# peeeeeeeep!

The match was about to start!

As the dinosaurs ran onto the pitch, Captain Custard couldn't believe his eyes. "Shiver me timbers!" he gasped. "You found your stuff!"

"And now we're ready to play football," Lightning said.

"F-f-football?" Captain Custard said,
his knees knocking,
his cutlass shaking.

"W-w-w-we never play football.
W-w-w-we only like to play tricks on people!"

And with that, the
Cowardly Custard Crew
legged it back to their ship.

"AwWW," Ziggy groaned.
"I was looking forward to chasing
those sea dogs round the pitch."

"Never mind," said Coco.
"We've already played a bit of football."

It was true. Dinosaurs United had done
some great **headers** and saved
loads of water balloon **goals**.
Not to mention **dribbling**
past lots of nippy crabs.

Lightning chuckled. "And we've got some pirate treasure –

# Custard doughnuts

## for everyone!

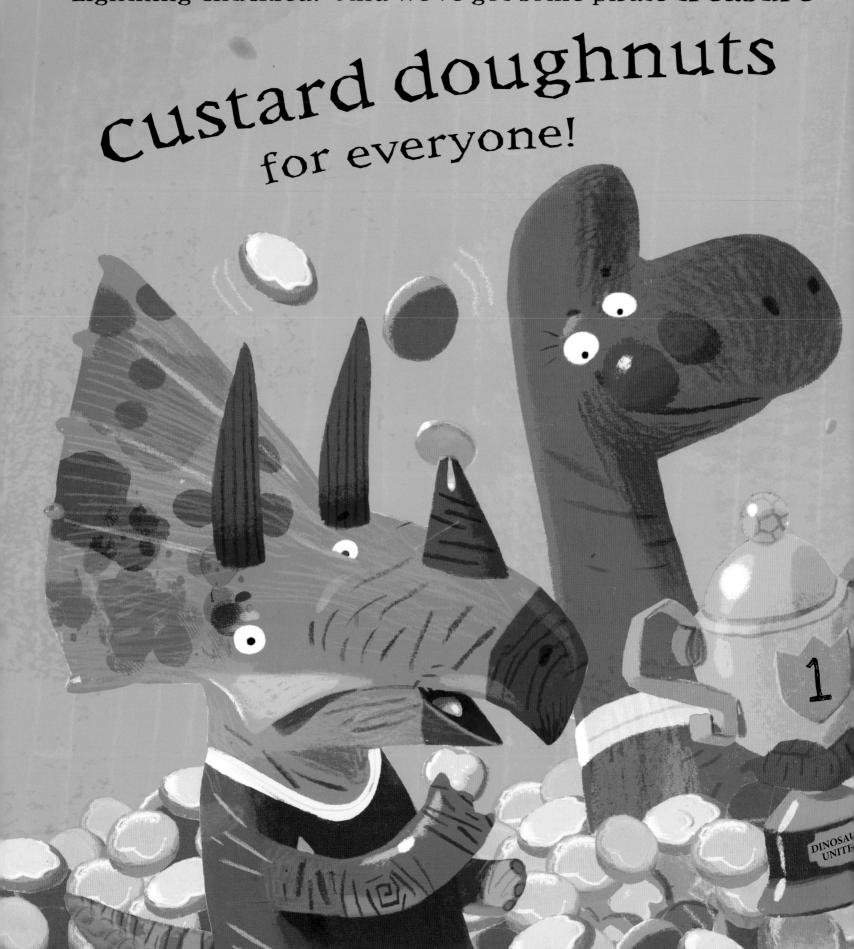

# I wish I could... ROAR!

## A story about self-confidence

Tiziana Bendall-Brunello

Illustrated by John Bendall-Brunello

QED

QED Publishing

"ROAR!" said Daddy Lion.
And all the little animals ran off in fright.

"Squeak!" said Little Lion.

ROAR

Squeak!

"Not squeak!" said Dad. "We lions ROAR! Now off you go and practise roaring. Keep practising... ROAR... ROAR... ROAR! I know you can do it."

Little Lion decided to practise
on his mum.
    "Squeak!" he called,
pouncing on her.

Squea

"It's not squeak!" said Mummy Lion. "It's ROAR!"

"Why don't you ask your brothers and sisters to show you how?"

"ROAR! ROAR! ROAR!
Roar! Roar! Roar!"
All Little Lion's brothers
and sisters were waking up
and roaring loudly.

ROAR!

"Squeak!" tried Little Lion
again. "Squeak, squeak!"

Squeak!

ROAR!

Roar!

Roar!

But the others just laughed at him.
"Not squeak!" they said. "ROAR!"

Little Lion ran away into the long grass.

"I wish I could roar," snuffled Little Lion. "But all I can do is..."

Squeak!

"Squeak!" said Mouse.

"Squeak!" said Little
Lion back to Mouse.

"Why are you squeaking?" asked Mouse.
"You lions roar – you don't squeak!
It's we mice that go squeak!" she said.

"Let me see if I can help you," said Mouse.

Squeak!

"It's no good," sniffled Little Lion. "I can't roar."

"Well, let's see if this helps," said Mouse.
And she whispered softly into his ear,
"ROAR! You can do it! ROAR!"

ROAR!

"Roar!" said Little Lion proudly.

"Hey!" Little Lion's brothers and sisters shouted proudly. "You've learned to roar! Hurrah! Hurrah!"

ROAR!

"We knew you could ROAR!" Daddy and Mummy Lion said. "You just didn't know that yourself."

"Yes, I can!" said Little Lion triumphantly. "ROAR! ROAR! ROAR!"

# Notes for parents and teachers

- Look at the front cover of the book together. Ask the children to name the animal. Can the children guess how the animal feels?

- Can the children understand the meaning of "ROAR" and "SQUEAK"? Show them the differences between a roar and a squeak. For this exercise, focus on your posture and facial expression. Discuss how you feel when you roar and squeak, and how other people may react to these two behaviours.

- Ask the children why Little Lion cries. Discuss reasons for crying and feelings associated with crying. Do the children know the opposite of crying? At this point, it is good to discuss with the children the different types of feelings (e.g. happy, sad) and associated behaviours and facial expressions.

- Ask the children why the other lions laugh at Little Lion. Is it a good thing to laugh when a friend is crying? Discuss ways in which children could help their friends when they cry.

- Can the children name all the animals in the book? Ask them which animal they like the most and why.

- Ask the children to describe what happens to the other animals when Little Lion says "ROAR". How does Little Lion look when he says "ROAR"?

- Ask the children to draw a picture of themselves saying "SQUEAK" and then saying "ROAR".

Consultant: Cecilia A. Essau
Professor of Developmental Psychopathology
Director of the Centre for Applied Research and
Assessment in Child and Adolescent Wellbeing,
Roehampton University, London

Editor: Jane Walker
Designer: Fiona Hajée

Copyright © QED Publishing 2011

First published in the UK in 2011 by
QED Publishing
A Quarto Group Company
226 City Road
London EC1V 2TT

www.qed-publishing.co.uk

A catalogue record for this book is available from the British Library.

ISBN 978 1 84835 728 0

Printed in China